A SCYTHE, A ROOSTER, AND A CAT

JANINA DOMANSKA

GREENWILLOW BOOKS

NEW YORK

Library of Congress Cataloging in Publication Data
Domanska, Janina. A scythe, a rooster, and a cat.   Summary: Adaptation of a Russian folktale about three brothers who make their fortunes, one with a scythe, one with a rooster, and one with a cat. [1. Folklore—Russia] I. Title.
PZ8.1.D717Sc   398.2'1'0947   [E]   80-17445   ISBN 0-688-80308-3   ISBN 0-688-84308-5 (lib. bdg.)

TO AVA WEISS WITH LOVE

In a village in Russia there lived a poor old man and his three sons: Vasily, Nikolai and Alexander. All he possessed was a scythe, a rooster and a cat. Before he died he gave the scythe to his youngest son Vasily, the rooster to the middle son Nikolai, and the cat to the eldest son Alexander.

Vasily took the scythe and set out in search of work. After a time he came to a village surrounded by fields of clover. It was harvest time and the villagers were gathering the clover by hand. When they saw the stranger carrying an odd-looking blade attached to a pole, they were frightened. They had never before seen a scythe.

"What is that you carry on your shoulder?" they asked.

"It is a scythe," Vasily replied.

"What is it for?" they asked.

"This scythe can cut the clover for you," Vasily said.

Some of the villagers hurried to the Boyar to tell him about the stranger and his scythe. The Boyar at once asked them to bring Vasily to the castle.

"I would like your scythe to cut my clover," the Boyar said. "I will pay whatever you ask."

"I would like two suppers, one for me and one for my scythe," Vasily replied. "You see, when my scythe is tired, it gets ravenously hungry."

The Boyar agreed, and promised to give Vasily a bag of golden rubles, as well, when the work was done.

Vasily ate the two suppers, and worked from sunset to sunrise, so that by morning most of the clover was cut. The Boyar and the villagers were delighted. The Boyar handed a bag of golden rubles to Vasily and said, "If you will leave the scythe with me, I will give you a bag filled with emeralds."

Vasily happily exchanged the scythe for the bag of emeralds, and left for home.

The villagers placed the scythe in a field that Vasily had not mown and brought it a delicious lunch of freshly baked black bread, milk and cheese. Then they went about their business.

But when the villagers came back later, the scythe had neither eaten the lunch nor cut the clover.

The Boyar was terribly disappointed. He ordered them to beat the scythe for its laziness, but nothing would make the scythe work.

Then a man picked up the scythe by its handle and made a sweeping motion with it in an effort to break it in two, but the scythe didn't break. Instead it cut the clover as it swept the field, and that is how the villagers learned to use a scythe.

Now it was Nikolai's turn to leave home. He took the rooster under his arm and was on his way. After walking a long distance, he came to a valley surrounded by high mountains. It was early morning and still dark and he was surprised to see that many people were gathered around a huge bonfire. They were all watching some men who were climbing the steep slopes of the mountain.

.

As Nikolai came up to the bonfire, his rooster suddenly crowed, "Cock-a-doodle-doo!"

"What's all this noise?" the people asked.

Nikolai saw that the sun was just coming up over the mountain. "My rooster is calling the sun up for you," he said.

The people took Nikolai and his rooster to the Prince. The Prince ordered that the rooster be given corn, and that a magnificent coop be built to house him. Thenceforth the rooster crowed from midnight till dawn, and the sun always came up, bringing light and warmth to the people. The Prince rewarded Nikolai with many treasures, and he too returned home a rich man.

Now it was Alexander's turn to go out into the world. He took the cat, said good-bye to his brothers, and started out. After many days of walking, he came to a city where the rich domes of churches glittered in the sunlight. But the city was overrun with rats, who had eaten all the grain in the granaries, and the people were hungry. When they saw the stranger and his cat, they asked, "What kind of animal is that?"

"It is a cat and it catches rats," replied Alexander.

"What good fortune that you have come," the people cried.

Alexander was led to the Tsar's palace. The Tsar looked doubtfully at the cat. He did not believe this strange animal could save his kingdom. Suddenly the cat meowed and jumped under the Tsar's throne. He soon came out with a rat in his mouth. The Tsar clapped his hands. "I'll give you this diamond ring and a casket of precious stones, if you give me your cat."

Alexander agreed. The cat drove the rats from the kingdom, and Alexander returned home with his treasures.

And after that all three brothers lived happily. They married, had children, and never knew what hunger meant.

DATE DUE

DEC 07 2015